The Skateboard Dare

A Novel by Nancy E. Krulik
Based on the Al Burton Production LASSIE
Adapted from the episode "The Skateboard Saga"
Written by Dave Meyer

BERKLEY BOOKS, NEW YORK

LASSIE: THE SKATEBOARD DARE

A Berkley Book / published by arrangement with
Palladium Media Enterprises, Inc.

PRINTING HISTORY
Berkley edition / March 1990

ISBN: 0-425-12119-4

A BERKLEY BOOK® TM 757,375
Berkley Books are published by The Berkley Publishing Group,
200 Madison Avenue, New York, New York 10016.
The name "Berkley" and the "B" logo
are trademarks belonging to Berkley Publishing Corporation.

PRINTED IN THE UNITED STATES OF AMERICA

10 9 8 7 6 5 4 3 2 1

For Hy and Lil

DAZZLING—OR DANGEROUS?

Hacksaw looked over and spotted Will and Lassie. "Well, look who's here," he called in a taunting voice. "Come on! Take a shot!"

"You got it!" Will called as he hopped on the skateboard and drove for the ramp. He could feel his excitement growing as he heard the skateboard slam onto the homemade ramp and then sail off it, flying in the air for just a second. Before he knew it, Will landed back on the ground again with a slam as the wheels of the skateboard smacked the pavement.

"All right, McCulloch!" one of the boys from Will's class cheered.

"Yeah, good one!" called another.

Hacksaw wasn't the least bit pleased with all the attention Will was getting. "Not bad," he said matter-of-factly. "But you didn't get enough air into it."

Lassie watched Will nervously from the sidelines. She didn't like the way the back wheel on the borrowed skateboard seemed to wobble back and forth. If the wheel dropped off the board in midflight, Will could slip from the board and really hurt himself.

"Ruff! Ruff!" Lassie tried to bark a warning to Will. But the boy was having too much fun to pay any attention to the message . . .

LASSIE ®

The Skateboard Dare

CHAPTER
1

WHOOSH! The skateboard soared off the steep homemade ramp at high speed. As the board hit the ground below, its rider bent his knees, raised his arms, and tilted his body slightly to the left to take the turn without falling. He stood slowly as he reached the end of the course, and the skateboard skidded to a stop.

"Yeah! All right!" The crowd of boys that had gathered to watch their friend ride his board on the ramp ran over to cheer him on.

"Nice going!"

"Awesome!"

"Hacksaw, you are the coolest!"

Hacksaw didn't even smile back at his adoring fans, never mind offer them a word of thanks. Hacksaw was a tough kid. He was twelve years old, about two years older than most of the other boys who had gathered at the homemade ramp. Hacksaw was an expert skateboarder, but he took too many chances. He always rode his board without wearing a helmet or protective pads, and he always set up dangerous homemade skateboard courses in unsafe places. It had been Hacksaw's idea to build the rickety, wobbly, quarter-pipe ramp he had just taken off from in the first place.

The boys had all worked together to build the ramp. Well, almost all of them. Hacksaw himself didn't do any of the physical labor. He stood off to the side barking orders to the others.

The ramp led right into a road that was closed off to traffic while it was being repaired. The road backed into an old reservoir which had been drained for the time being, so the workmen could complete their work on the road.

When Hacksaw was through showing off on the ramp, he decided to demonstrate his talents by skating along the base of the reservoir that stood at the end of the road. The reservoir was blocked off by a chainlink fence, but Hacksaw found a part of the fence that had been knocked down by the wind and could be climbed over easily. Some of the younger boys hadn't wanted to climb over the rickety old aluminum chainlink fence. But Hacksaw had dared them to climb it, and because none of the boys wanted to be called a chicken, they had all followed the older boy over the fence and into the reservoir.

So within a few minutes, most of the boys were happily skateboarding around the base of the reservoir at top speed, shrieking with delight. Some of the more experienced skateboarders were taking off from the upper lip of the reservoir and attempting daring midair poses before landing in the base of the reservoir.

Ten-year-old Will McCulloch and his faithful brown and white purebred collie, Lassie, stood on the other side of the chainlink fence, watching the kids as they rode. Will stared enviously at the group of laughing, shouting skateboarders.

"Lucky guys," he said with more than just a touch of jealousy in his voice. Will loved riding skateboards. Unfortunately, right now his board was broken.

Lassie rubbed up against her master's leg and whined. Will looked down at Lassie and petted the soft white spot at the top of her head. "Forget it, Lassie," he said with a laugh. "You're not getting on any skateboard."

Will pulled his bike up closer to the fence to get a better look at the quarter-pipe ramp. Lassie followed close at his heels. As Will stuck his face up against the metal fence, he was met by Hacksaw's icy stare.

"Better not get too close," Hacksaw said, laughing mockingly. "You might get hurt."

It was all Will could do to manage a small, shaky smile back at Hacksaw. Will wasn't afraid of getting hurt by a runaway skateboard. He was more afraid of getting hurt by this older bully who was staring him down.

Hacksaw laughed again and then took off to skate around the base. Will watched the kids ride for a while. He was so engrossed in their moves that he didn't even notice when Lassie left his side and trotted a few yards up the side of the hill.

"Ruff! Ruff!" Lassie called to Will.

Will turned toward his dog. "What is it, girl?" Will called up to her as he walked his bike over to Lassie to get a good look at what had upset her so.

"Ruff! Ruff!" Lassie barked again, using her head to point to a small, ground-level concrete flood channel that held the water back from the reservoir.

Will looked from the channel to the skateboarders. "I know it's dangerous," he admitted to Lassie. "But sometimes you have to look the other way. Besides, I'm sure someone will warn those kids before they open the channel and let the water back in the reservoir." Will looked at the laughing boys one more time. Then sadly, he hopped on his bike and started to ride back to the main road. "Come on," he called to Lassie.

The boy rode slowly down the road toward his house with his happy collie running right beside him. Lassie loved running alongside Will when he rode his bicycle. She loved the feeling of the wind as it rushed through her shiny brown and white fur. She loved the feeling of the soft dirt road beneath her paws. Most of all, Lassie loved spending time with Will. It always made her very happy.

But Will was not happy at all. "Of all the times not to have a skateboard," he murmured sadly to Lassie. "I know one thing. When I get a new one, I'm going to take great care of it. And I'm not going to let anyone borrow it, either!"

At the end of the road, Will came upon three bright orange traffic cones that blocked any cars from going down the street toward the reservoir. A sign looped over the center cone warned in big white letters: ROAD TEMPORARILY CLOSED FOR CONSTRUCTION. Will hoped the construction would go on long enough for him to have a chance to try a few skateboard wheelies with the other kids.

Back at the McCullochs's house, Will's fourteen-year-old sister, Megan, was sitting in the living room doing her algebra homework.

She sat sideways in a big, overstuffed easy chair, with her legs stretched over one arm of the chair and her long blonde hair draped over the other arm. Their mother, Dee, was doing some work at her desk. Dee owned a personnel business. She matched up interested workers with companies that could use their services. It was a convenient business because Dee could do most of the work from her desk in the living room of her home. Dee looked over at her daughter from across the room and frowned.

"After about fifteen minutes you might want to shift your legs over to the other side. That way you'll wear out the chair more evenly," Dee teased Megan.

"Good idea," Megan said with a smile, as she played along with her mother's teasing.

"Or possibly, you might even want to sit the regular way. Who knows? It might even be more comfortable."

Megan looked down at her algebra book and groaned. "When you're doing homework," she grumbled, "no way is comfortable."

Dee looked at Megan and shrugged. She was about to go back to work when her husband Chris came storming down the stairs and into the living room.

"I can't believe this telephone bill!" he bellowed, waving the blue and white papers in the air. "Look at all these calls to San Diego!" He held the bill out in front of him and looked down the list of long-distance numbers. "Area code 619 . . . area code 619 . . . 619 . . . 619 . . . !" Annoyed, he handed the bill over to Dee for a look.

Dee scanned the bill for a while and looked over at Megan. "I think most of these were to Megan's friend Becky."

"That's what I was afraid of." Chris sighed.

Megan got up from her chair and walked over to her mother. "Let me see that," she said, taking the bill. "Yep, that's Becky's number all right." Megan wasn't the least bit surprised. She knew that most of the calls would be to her old friend from San Diego. The McCullochs had moved north to suburban Glen Ridge, California, from San Diego only a few months ago and Megan was still attached to her friends in the old neighborhood. Not that she hadn't made lots of friends in Glen Ridge. She had met a lot of people by getting involved in various school activities like the photography club. She had even become the mascot for the Glen Ridge High School cheerleaders! But no matter how many friends Megan made in suburban Glen Ridge, she was still attached to her old city pals.

"This is terrible," Chris groaned as he slumped into a chair and looked once again at the costly phone bill.

"Sweetheart, don't worry," Dee consoled him. "Megan and I will talk about this."

"No, I mean I feel terrible," Chris said without looking up.

Megan giggled. "You're supposed to. That's what dads do. They get upset about phone bills." She laughed.

Chris took a deep breath. "What I am saying is that it's all my fault. If I hadn't moved my construction business out of San Diego and dragged us up here to Glen Ridge . . ."

". . . to live with a bunch of hicks," Megan interrupted him.

"Megan!" Dee scolded. She really got annoyed when Megan talked like a city snob.

"Come on, Mom," Megan teased. "Dad doesn't feel guilty all that often. You've got to take advantage of it when you can."

But Chris didn't see any humor in the situation at all. He looked at Dee through guilt-ridden eyes. "Don't you see what I've done?" he asked his wife. "In order to have any friends, my daughter is forced to live in the past."

"Look, Will has already made friends here. For that matter, so has Megan." Dee shot her daughter an aggravated glance. "That phone is always ringing for you," she said to Megan.

Before Megan could respond, Will came

slumping into the living room with Lassie padding close behind.

"Hi, Will," Chris said glumly from his chair.

"Hi," Will mumbled. "You are looking at a man with a problem."

"So are you," Chris replied good-naturedly.

"You know that little road that runs next to the reservoir?" Will continued, ignoring his father's comment. "Well, it's closed for construction. Some of the kids have set up the coolest skateboard ramp. It's the perfect place—no cars!"

Dee grew concerned. "Are you sure you are ready for a ramp?" she asked. "It's been a while since I've seen you on your skateboard."

"What skateboard?" Will harrumphed. "I lent mine to Petey Morhead and he left it in his driveway . . . That's my problem. Petey's dad accidentally backed his car over it!"

Chris choked back a laugh. "I trust nobody was on it at the time?" He smiled.

"Dad this is serious! I need a skateboard now! That road could be reopened any day."

"I doubt it," Chris assured him. "I think that street will probably be ripped up for weeks."

But Will wouldn't be consoled. "Do you realize Tim Milford and I are the only two boys in class without skateboards?"

Dee had had just about enough of Will's complaining. "Will, please. Your father can't take any more guilt," she said sternly.

Megan looked up from her algebra homework. "Will, what are you talking about?" she asked. "Tim Milford has a skateboard. I've seen him on it."

"Not lately," Will explained. "His parents grounded him because of his Social Studies grades." Will smiled suddenly. He had a great idea. After a beat he added, "Hey! Knowing Milford, it'll be forever before he gets that grade up. Maybe I can borrow his skateboard."

Dee walked back over to her desk and picked up a pencil. "Problem solved," she said as she looked back down at her paperwork.

"I'll ask him tomorrow after school," Will said gleefully.

"Speaking of Social Studies," Chris remarked, knowing full well he had interrupted his son. "That paper on the Egyptian pyramids is due on the eighteenth, isn't it? That's just three days away."

Will looked at the floor. "I'm basically finished," he said matter-of-factly.

"Basically?" Chris questioned him.

"I just have a few odds and ends to clear up."

"Maybe you could start working on some of

those 'odds and ends' right now," Chris suggested without really giving Will any choice.

Will was about to argue, but one look at his father's face made him change his mind. With a sigh, Will got up and walked to the stairs that led to his room, with Lassie following close behind.

CHAPTER
2

The very next day, as soon as the three-thirty school bell rang, Will ran outside to catch Tim Milford in the school playground before he headed home. Will wanted to ask Tim to loan him his skateboard for a while. As Will crossed the playground to catch up with Tim, visions of homemade pipe ramps and airborne skateboard maneuvers raced through his brain. Finally Will caught up to Tim and his pal Josh on the street that led to the school.

"Hey, Milford! Wait up!" Will called through breathless gasps. Tim and Josh stopped midstep and turned to wait for Will.

"So, Milford," Will asked hesitantly, "you still grounded because of your Social Studies exam?"

Tim kicked at the ground with the toe of his

black canvas high-top sneaker. "Yeah," he answered defensively. "Why?"

"I was just wondering, well . . . uh . . . I mean, since you can't use it or anything, you think maybe I could borrow your skateboard for a little bit?" Will asked, trying not to sound too eager.

"I don't know," Tim said. "I've put a lot of money into this board. New trucks, new rails, grip tape . . ."

Will got very excited. "Oh, man! New trucks and rails!" he interrupted, shouting.

Josh patted Tim on the shoulder. "Why not loan it to him? Staring at the board in your room and not being able to use it is driving you bonkers anyway."

Will shot Josh a grateful glance.

"That's true," Tim began, "but . . ."

Will didn't let him finish. "Great! So you'll do it?" Will squealed, slapping Tim on the back. Will jumped up and down with delight. In his excitement, Will dropped his notebook. His papers went flying all over the place. Tim and Josh bent down to help Will pick them up.

"Hey, look at this," Tim said to Josh, holding up a folder of papers. "This isn't due until October eighteenth! Today's only the sixteenth!

Leave it to a brain like McCulloch to have his Egyptian pyramids paper done two days early."

Will could feel his face burning red with embarrassment. "I guess Social Studies just comes easily to me." He shrugged.

"Come on," Josh urged Tim. "We've got to get going."

Tim ignored Josh. "Hold on a second," he said turning to Will. "You want to borrow my skateboard, right?" Tim asked.

Will nodded, confused.

"Okay, I'll make you a deal," Tim explained. "I'll lend you my skateboard for a whole week and in return you write my Social Studies paper for me."

Will looked stunned. He hadn't planned on having to trade anything for the skateboard—especially not a homework assignment!

"Gee, I don't know," Will began.

"For a smart guy like you, McCulloch, a few pages on the pyramids is nothing," Tim said, smiling.

"Yeah . . . but . . ."

"Okay, fine," Tim said, bluffing. "It was just an idea. Let's go Josh . . ."

Once again Will had visions of the closed off road, the skateboard ramp, and the other kids riding along the reservoir. He just had to have that skateboard!

"Okay, I'll do it," Will said quickly as he grabbed Tim's shoulder to stop him from leaving.

"Great!" Tim smiled. He put out his hand and Will took it. The two boys shook solemnly on the deal.

"Remember who you're writing it for. Better throw in a lot of mistakes to make it look real." Josh laughed. Tim gave his pal a dirty look.

"You bring in my paper tomorrow and I'll give you the skateboard," Tim said over his shoulder as he and Josh left to walk home.

"You bet!" Will shouted after him as he ran home to get started.

That night, right after supper, Will raced up to his room and turned on his computer to write Tim's Social Studies paper. Lassie sat by the side of Will's chair watching him curiously.

The collie was very disappointed. Usually right after dinner, Will would play with Lassie for an hour or two. The two pals would wrestle on the living room floor, or play fetch out in the backyard, or just sit quietly watching TV while Will brushed Lassie's thick, gleaming, brown and white coat with a bristly wire dog brush.

But tonight, Will hadn't taken any time to play with Lassie at all. He had run up to his room to write this paper. No one else in the family had noticed it, but Will seemed just a little nervous about this paper. Lassie was very sensitive to Will's behavior, and she could sense that deep down the boy was uncomfortable with what he was doing. Will could fool anyone but Lassie. Of course, Lassie couldn't know that Will was writing a paper for someone else, but she could sense that whatever Will was doing, it was wrong.

Will opened the encyclopedia to "Egypt" and started to type. "The . . . pyramids . . . of . . . Egypt . . . evolved in the . . . fourth dynasty . . ." he said softly to himself as he typed.

Lassie used her teeth to pick up a small, red rubber ball from under Will's bed. She carried the ball in her mouth until she reached the desk. Then, without a sound, Lassie dropped the ball on Will's desk. With a quick extra motion, Lassie used her long pointed nose to shut the encyclopedia. She wanted to play!

Will steadied the ball on the desk right next to his computer. "Hey, come on," he scolded Lassie. "I've got to get this done. Now don't bug me!"

Will flipped the pages of the encyclopedia until he found his place. Then he laid the book out flat and began typing again. "Each . . . monarch . . . constructed . . . his own pyramid . . ." he typed, "to preserve . . . his mummified . . . body . . . for eternity . . ."

Will didn't turn around, but he could still feel Lassie's icy stare on his back. Finally, he turned in his chair to answer her stern look.

"Look, Lassie," he explained, "this isn't really cheating. It's just . . . just helping a friend."

Lassie held her stare. Something in Will's tone of voice told her that he didn't really believe what he was telling her.

"See, cheating would be if I was having Tim write the paper for me. But since I'm doing it for him . . . it's just a favor."

Lassie shook her head and barked sternly at Will.

"Okay, I'm getting a skateboard out of it . . . But it's only for a week."

Will turned back to his computer. But before he could type one word, Lassie padded over to the computer and put her paws on the desk next to Will. Standing only on her hind legs, Lassie reached up with her paw to bat the red ball from the desk. When she moved, the collie hit the keyboard with her paw.

Will watched in shock as the computer screen went blank. "Lassie!" he shouted in panic as he frantically started hitting the keys on the keyboard, trying to retrieve Tim's report.

"You wiped out my whole report!" he

shouted at the dog. Frustrated, Will got up and took Lassie by the collar. "That's it!" he yelled. "You are out of here!" Then he dragged her down the stairs to the family room.

"Effective immediately," Will announced to his parents, "my room is off limits to Lassie!"

Dee looked up questioningly from her desk. "Off limits?" she asked.

"She just hit my computer and lost my . . . homework," Will explained, stumbling just slightly over the last word.

"Bad dog!" Dee scolded Lassie.

The collie looked up at Will through sad, slanted eyes for a reprieve. But Will avoided her eyes. "Now I'm going to have to start all over again," was all he said.

"Well, don't worry, we won't let her near your room," Chris said. "Lassie, come. Sit," he ordered the dog.

Ever obedient, Lassie moped over to the couch and sat at Chris's feet. She watched with disappointment as Will dashed out of the family room and back up the stairs to his room.

Megan passed her younger brother on the stairs on her way into the family room. "If one of you goes out tonight, could you mail this for me?" she asked her parents as she entered the room, waving a lavender envelope in the air.

"Sure." Chris smiled, taking the envelope from her.

"I want to be sure Becky gets it right away," she said.

Chris looked curiously at the envelope. "There's no stamp on here," he observed.

Megan smiled proudly. "I know. That way we save on the phone bill and on the price of a stamp," she explained. "Becky did it on her letter to me, too. I put her name and address on the back and mine on the front. Then when the post office stamps it 'Insufficient Postage—Return to Sender,' it'll go right to Becky."

Chris shook his head in disbelief. "Megan," he said, "this is crazy—not to mention probably illegal."

"What happens if it comes back to you?" Dee asked. "After all, your zip code is closer."

"I'm desperate to hear from someone from San Diego. I'll read it anyhow," Megan said grinning.

"Forget it." Chris was not amused. "Go put a stamp on it," he said, handing the envelope back to Megan.

Chris's sad eyes followed his daughter as she left the room. Then he sat down on the couch and looked at Dee. "Megan's right about one thing, though." He sighed.

"What's that?"

"I have made her a desperate woman. I know this just sounds like a case of mover's re-morse, but I can't help feeling that if we hadn't moved up here, away from her old friends, she'd be hanging out at the mall in San Diego with Becky and her other old friends right now . . ."

Dee smiled gently and moved over to the couch to cuddle up close to her husband. "You're just being hard on yourself. Megan could be hanging out at the Glen Ridge Mall right now with any one of her new friends if she really wanted to."

"Maybe," Chris murmured, unconvinced.

CHAPTER
3

The following day, Will had a tough time paying attention in school. Every time he opened his looseleaf notebook to take notes on the lifestyles of the ancient Egyptians, he found himself doodling pictures of skateboards instead of pyramids. More than once he caught himself staring out the window, daydreaming about doing axle stalls on Tim's skateboard.

Finally school let out. Will met up with Tim and Josh on the same street they'd been on the afternoon before. Will peeked around to make sure no one was watching them or listening in on their conversation. When he was sure the coast was clear, he pulled a red folder holding six white pieces of computer paper out of his notebook and handed it to Tim.

"There you go," Will said proudly. "Six

solid pages, double spaced. I even threw in a run-on sentence or two, plus a couple of spelling errors to make it look good."

Tim flipped through the pages absentmindedly. "I'll take your word for it," he said. "I can't read this stuff."

Josh reached over and closed the folder. "He's an A student. It's got to be good," Josh assured Tim impatiently. "Just give him the board and let's get out of here!"

Tim nodded in agreement. "You wouldn't happen to know anything about ninth grade Spanish, would you?" he asked Will.

Will eyed the skateboard hungrily. He was starting to get annoyed. What did Tim want from him now?"

"Spanish? Afraid not," Will said quickly, staring at the neon green board tucked under Tim's right arm.

"If my brother doesn't get his grade up to a D he's going to be kicked off the Junior Varsity football team," Tim explained.

Will's eyes grew bright. "Oh, sure, your brother is Steve Milford, the star wide receiver on the Glen Ridge High Junior Varsity team," Will said enviously. It must be really neat to have a star football player for an older brother, instead of a sister who liked taking pictures all the time, Will thought.

"With a one point three grade point average," Tim said and laughed, jabbing Josh in the ribs. Will didn't see what was so funny. A one point three grade point average meant that Steve Milford got almost straight Ds on his report card!

"Have Steve call my sister, Megan. She's a wiz in Spanish. She might be able to find a few minutes to help him," Will said helpfully.

"Great!" Tim smiled. "Here's my board," he said, handing Will the green neon skateboard. "Take care of it."

Will reached for the board greedily, unable to disguise how thrilled he was at getting his hands on such a terrific skateboard. "Thanks. I'll have it back in one week," he promised breathlessly. Then, too excited to stand around talking anymore, Will charged off toward his house to change into his old jeans.

"Later maybe we can make a deal for you to do my science project!" Tim called after Will.

Josh looked at Tim and shook his head. "By the way," he asked, "did you remember to get that loose wheel fixed before you gave the board to Will?"

Tim opened his eyes wide and shook his head. "Oops, forgot," he said. Tim watched Josh shake his head again. "I had that dumb Social Studies paper on my mind," he tried to excuse

27

himself, "and, well, it's no big deal. Will's just a little guy. It's not like he's going to shred the reservoir or anything."

"I guess he'll be fine," Josh said, shrugging his shoulders.

As soon as he got home, Will made his usual stop into the kitchen for a few double chocolate chip cookies and a glass of milk. Lassie was so excited to see him that she jumped up high on her hind legs and licked Will right on the nose. Then she followed him around the kitchen, her tail wagging wildly all the way, and watched hungrily as the boy reached into the box for his cookies.

"You want one, too?" Will asked Lassie, pointing to his cookies.

As her answer, Lassie wagged her tail even harder. Will smiled at her, then reached under the sink and pulled out a box of tan-colored, bone-shaped doggie biscuits. "This bone's yours." He laughed as he handed her the dog cookie. When his glass was drained and his cookies were eaten, Will went up the stairs to change his clothes. His faithful collie followed close behind him.

Downstairs in the family room, Megan was talking on the phone. She was in her usual sideways position in the overstuffed easy chair, with a textbook open in her lap and the phone receiver tucked tight between her right ear and her right shoulder.

"Yo voy, tú vas, él o ella va, nosotros vamos, ustedes van, ellas o ellos van," she said into the receiver.

Chris and Dee walked into the room as she was speaking. They watched as Megan listened to the party on the other end of the phone, smiled brightly, and then said, "Great. See you then. Bye!"

Chris laughed as his daughter hung up the phone. "Megan, you don't have to talk to your friends in code," he teased, knowing full well she was speaking in Spanish.

"Just practicing Spanish verbs with Steve Milford," Megan explained. "Dad, I have to make one more call to San Diego," she added sweetly.

"No more return-to-sender letters?" Chris teased.

"This is too important for a letter. I want to tell Becky all about Steve. I promised to study with him Saturday. If he doesn't get his Spanish grade up, he's off the team. And he's the star player!" Megan spouted out, all in one breath.

"But isn't Steve Milford just another 'hick'?" Dee asked with a sarcastic smirk. "What about all your city friends in San Diego?"

"Oh, Becky's still my best friend, that's why I want to call her," Megan assured her mother. "But San Diego is yesterday. After all, I live in Glen Ridge now. I should be hanging out with my friends from here."

Dee put her arm around Chris's waist as they watched Megan run upstairs to make her phone call in private.

"If Steve Milford stays on the team, they should give Megan a Junior Varsity letter," Dee said, giggling.

Just then Will came running down the steps, skateboard in hand. "I'm off," he called to his parents. "Refer all my calls to the skateboard ramp."

Before Will could get out the door, Lassie came running up beside him, holding his helmet by the strap between her teeth. Will tried to wave the dog away, but she plopped the helmet down on the floor right in front of him.

Dee walked over and petted the collie gratefully along her broad golden brown back. "Look at that. Skateboard helmet and pads. You never forget anything. Good girl," Dee complimented her.

Will was less than pleased. He was hoping to sneak out without his helmet and pads. After all, what would a cool big kid like Hacksaw think of a helmet and pads?

30

"Yeah, good going," Will said to Lassie in a most unconvincing manner. With a resigned sigh, Will bent down and picked up the helmet and pads.

"Will, when you get home, there may not be anyone here, so take your keys," Dee told him. "Dad and I are going to pick up the 4×4 in the shop, and we're dropping Megan off at the library."

"No problem," Will answered. Then he rushed out the door before anything or anyone else could stop him.

As soon as he and Lassie were outside, Will stopped to scold Lassie. "First you wipe out my report on the computer, and now this," he said angrily, holding up the helmet. "Who's side are you on, anyhow?"

Lassie whined a quiet sigh and rubbed up against Will's leg lovingly to show that she was always on his side, no matter what. She just wanted to make sure he was safe! Will sighed and put on his helmet and pads. When he was finished, he hooked Lassie's long leather leash up to her collar. Then, holding on to Lassie's leash, Will hopped on the skateboard and let the dog tow him through the streets to the reservoir.

Finally, the boy and his dog reached the blocked off street. Lassie led Will between two of the three rubber orange cones that blocked

off the street and over to the ramp. Will watched excitedly as some of the boys did Japan Airs, Mc-Twists, and Drop Ins in the air. Will felt a little better about his safety equipment when he saw that all the boys—except for Hacksaw—were wearing their helmets and kneepads. He might not look as cool as Hacksaw, but at least he didn't look like a weirdo.

Hacksaw looked over and spotted Will and Lassie. "Well, look who's here," he called in a taunting voice. "Come on! Take a shot!"

Will jumped off the skateboard, flipped it up in the air with his toe and caught it expertly with his right hand. "You got it!" he called as he ran down the street and over to the ramp.

When he was a few feet from the ramp, Will hopped on the skateboard and drove for the ramp. He could feel his excitement growing as he heard the skateboard slam onto the home-made ramp and then sail off it, flying in the air for just a second. Before he knew it, Will landed back on the ground again with a slam as the wheels of the skateboard smacked the pave-ment.

"All right, McCulloch!" one of the boys from Will's class at school complimented him on his jump.

"Yeah, good one!" called another.

Hacksaw wasn't the least bit pleased with

all the attention Will was getting. He was used to having all the compliments for himself. "Not bad," he said matter-of-factly. "But you didn't get enough air into it."

Lassie watched Will nervously from the sidelines. She didn't like the way the back wheel on the borrowed skateboard seemed to wobble back and forth. If the wheel dropped off the board in midflight, Will could slip from the board and really hurt himself.

"Ruff! Ruff!" Lassie tried to bark a warning to Will. But the boy was having too much fun to pay any attention to the message.

CHAPTER
4

One by one, the boys took turns taking off from the ramp and trying new aerial stunts. Hacksaw showed off for the crowd by taking off from the ramp and landing with one leg bent low to the ground and the other extended in a perfect "shoot the duck" style.

The older boy smirked slightly as the other boys cheered him on. But he turned and faced the ramp as Will raced toward it. Hacksaw stared daringly at Will as if to say, "Top that—I dare you!"

Will tried to keep his concentration on his skateboard, although it was hard for him to take his eyes off Hacksaw's menacing scowl. Will could feel the pressure in the air. All eyes were on him as he took off from the ramp. He was so tense, he barely felt the back wheel of the board shake beneath him. He closed his eyes tight as the board smashed into the ground with a powerful impact. Then, without taking a single breath, Will threw up his arms, jumped off his skateboard, turned in the air, and landed back on his board again. Will took a huge breath of relief as his board skidded to a stop. He'd done a perfect spinner!

"Whew!"

"Nice one, McCulloch!"

"Way to go, McCulloch!"

All at once the other boys were surrounding Will, patting him on the back in congratulations! Looking at the scene, Hacksaw could feel the anger and jealousy race through his body.

"Yeah, well watch this," he called to the crowd.

"Sorry, Hacksaw, I gotta get going," Timmy Mullholland said.

"Yeah, me, too," Joey Smith announced.

It was getting dark. Now that it was already October, 17th, the sun was beginning to set much earlier, limiting the amount of time the boys had to play. Many of the boys had to go home for dinner. Eventually it was only Will and Hacksaw alone by the ramp.

"I get the feeling you think you're pretty hot on that skateboard," Hacksaw said challengingly to Will.

"Not really," Will replied modestly.

"Well, maybe you wouldn't feel so secure on that board if you weren't wearing all that wimpy crash clothing," Hacksaw teased.

Will knew he shouldn't take off his helmet and pads. But he just couldn't let Hacksaw think he was a baby. Slowly, Will unfastened his knee-pads.

"Actually, this stuff does sort of get in my way," he said in his most matter-of-fact voice.

Lassie had been watching this whole scene from a distance. After Will had ignored her warning, she'd kept quiet. But this was too much! It was too dangerous for Will to be skating without his safety equipment! Lassie loved Will more than anything in the world. She felt it was her duty to protect him. After all, Will was Lassie's best friend.

"RUFF! RUFF!" Lassie called frantically to Will.

"Quiet!" Hacksaw shouted to Lassie.

Will glared at Hacksaw. Who did this kid think he was, yelling at Lassie like that? Well, Will would show him who was boss! Angrily, Will threw his helmet to the ground.

Laughing, Hacksaw raced up to the ramp, and in seconds exploded in the air, landing with one leg slightly bent on the board and the other straight out. Hacksaw smiled triumphantly as his board tipped backward in a perfect one-foot nose wheelie.

"Bet you can't do that," Hacksaw snarled. Will got very tense. He had never tried landing on one foot before.

"RUFF RUFF!" Lassie barked again.

"Get out of here, you," Hacksaw shouted at Lassie.

That was all it took to get Will going. He would show this bully a thing or two! He raced to the ramp. As he flew through the air, Will was sure his heart had stopped beating. But when he landed on the ground, his working leg was bent slightly, his other leg was pointed out, and his board miraculously tilted backward. He had done it! Maybe his wheelie didn't have the same style as Hacksaw's, but it was certainly okay!

"Ah, this is too easy," Hacksaw said. "Come on. Let's take on that reservoir!"

As Hacksaw moved up the hill he motioned for Will to follow him. Will followed Hacksaw without looking at Lassie. He couldn't stand to look at Lassie now. He knew the dog disapproved of what he was doing, and if there was one thing he couldn't stand, it was Lassie's disapproval.

Will was so determined to keep up with Hacksaw as he climbed the hill that he didn't even notice the bright orange sign that hung from the chainlink fence. CAUTION: RESERVOIR WILL BE REOPENED OCTOBER 17 the sign warned in bold white letters.

As they climbed higher and higher, Will got nervous. "I really don't think we should go in there," Will said tentatively.

Hacksaw laughed heartily. "Are you kidding? Everybody skateboards in here. It's no big deal—unless, of course, you're chicken . . ."

Will wasn't sure why he needed to prove himself to Hacksaw. He just did. So, reluctantly, Will followed Hacksaw as he climbed over the fence.

Lassie was left outside the fence. She watched nervously as Will followed Hacksaw to a steep part of the reservoir.

"This is a good place . . . I'll let you go first this time," Hacksaw told Will.

Will looked down the slope into the base of the reservoir. He seemed so far from the ground.

"Oh, that's okay," Will said nervously. "You can go first. After all, you're more familiar with—"

Hacksaw was growing impatient. "Hey," he said threateningly, moving closer to Will. "I said, you go first. I went first the last time. Fair is fair!"

Will backed away. "Okay," he said unconvincingly. "Sure . . . fair is . . . fair."

Will made his way to the lip of the reservoir and placed his board in position. He stood perfectly still for a couple of seconds as he set himself evenly on the board.

Will shut his eyes and held his breath. Then, in one swift motion he pushed off with his left leg. The next thing he knew, Will was racing down the reservoir at top speed, the wind blowing through the hair on his now unprotected head. Lassie watched breathlessly as Will reached the bottom of the reservoir and came up the other side doing an almost perfect axle twist.

Hacksaw followed, making the exact same motions as Will. When the two boys met up again, Will said a sincere "Nice going," to the older boy.

Hacksaw muttered an insincere "Thank you."

"Let's try it from over there," Hacksaw said to Will, pointing to an even higher part of the reservoir.

Will looked at the steepness of the slope. He got really scared. "Maybe we should stop now," he said, almost pleadingly. "I think it's starting to get dark."

"I'm not scared of the dark. Are you?" Hacksaw taunted.

"No, but . . ."

"Good," Hacksaw said, ending the discussion. "This time I'll go first."

Lassie watched as the boys moved farther up the hill. The wise collie knew Will was not experienced enough to ride the board from there—especially not with a shaky back wheel. Quickly she ran to the low part of the fence and tried to leap over it. But although she leaped as high as her collie legs would go, Lassie couldn't get enough height to jump over the fence. She was forced to give up. Frantically, Lassie charged up the hill, barking a warning to Will.

When they reached the top, Will looked at Hacksaw. "You sure you want to do this, Hacksaw?" he asked, his voice shaking. "It's pretty steep here."

Hacksaw didn't reply. He just sneered at Will. Then the bully set himself solidly on his board, kicked off, and went speeding down the hill faster than Will had ever seen anyone move on a skateboard. Will watched with genuine admiration as the bigger boy angled down the steep side of the reservoir and banked around the curved corner, picking up just enough momentum to send himself gliding up the adjoining wall. Will was about to applaud when suddenly, Hacksaw lost control of his skateboard. The board slipped out from under him at top speed!

Will ran down the hill toward Hacksaw.
Lassie followed his movements from her side of
the fence. When Will reached Hacksaw, he noticed a trickle of a tear coming from the boy's
eye. Hacksaw was really in pain.

"It's my leg . . ." Hacksaw began, clutching
at his calf.

Will wanted to say, "Not bad but you didn't
get enough air into it," just as Hacksaw had
done to him, but seeing the boy lying there in
pain, Will didn't have the heart. Instead, he bent
over and looked at Hacksaw's leg. "Okay, just
try to take it easy and we'll get you out of here,"
Will said calmly.

"How? I can't walk," Hacksaw snarled.

Will stopped to think. "Good question," he
answered slowly. Will looked up. The sun was
setting rapidly. It was getting dark. Before long,
the two boys would be stuck all alone in the dark
at the bottom of the reservoir!

Lassie was desperate to get to Will. Using
her sharp nails to dig, the resourceful collie dug
a hole under the fence, deep enough for her to
crawl through. Before he knew it, Lassie was at
Will's side, offering her assistance.

"Good girl, Lassie." Will smiled, petting
her.

"That's all we need," Hacksaw moaned. "A
dog."

Will ignored him. "Maybe she can help," Will thought out loud. "Hold on to her collar," he ordered Hacksaw.

"What!" Hacksaw shouted at Will.

"Just hold on to her collar!" Will repeated.

Hacksaw was in no position to argue. He took hold of the collar and, with Lassie pulling and Will pushing, the two tried to roll Hacksaw up the reservoir. They struggled bravely, but the hill was just too steep.

"RUFF! RUFF! RUFF!" Lassie barked her most ferocious warning bark.

"What is it, Lassie?" Will said, alarmed by the severity of her barks. Lassie motioned toward the top of the reservoir with her head.

"Oh, no!" Will cried out in fear. Water was rushing down the side of the reservoir from the flood channel.

"They've opened the flood channel. This place is going to be full of water before we know it!"

CHAPTER
5

"I'll drown!" Hacksaw cried out in a voice filled with fear and desperation. "I can't swim!" The older boy looked at Will through pleading, frightened eyes. "Do something. Get your parents."

His mother's words raced through Will's mind. "When you get home there may not be anyone here . . ."

"They're not home," Will said quickly to Hacksaw.

Hacksaw fidgeted nervously as he watched Will standing quietly and studying the open flood channel. The now vulnerable bully shouted loudly as Will started to walk up the steep slope of the reservoir to the channel.

"Where are you going? Are you going to just leave me here?"

"Stay right here," Will ordered Hacksaw.

Hacksaw looked down at his swollen leg. "Where am I gonna go?" he asked sarcastically.

Will ignored the comment. "Keep an eye on him, Lassie," was all he said before he left.

Left alone together, Lassie and Hacksaw eyed each other with resentment. Neither one was too fond of the other.

Will ran up the side of the reservoir at top speed. He climbed over the fence in one continuous movement. He knew he didn't have much time. Rapidly, Will ran over to the closed-off road and grabbed the makeshift skateboard ramp. The ramp was heavy, and it took more strength than Will ever knew he had to drag it up the hill and over to the spot where the flood gate emptied the gallons of fast flowing water into the reservoir. Will turned the skateboard ramp on its side and shoved it across the spillway so that the water was redirected away from the reservoir and off to the side. Will turned and braced himself against the ramp to make sure that the water wouldn't force itself past the ramp and go rushing into the reservoir.

"Lassie! Here, Lassie!" Will called to his dog from his post at the flood channel.

At the sound of her master's voice, Lassie left Hacksaw's side and went tearing up the side of the reservoir. She climbed through the hole she had dug under the fence, and ran right for Will.

"Good girl," Will said as calmly as he could. Will was having a tough time remaining calm. Despite his efforts, some of the water was spilling into the reservoir, and the water level at the bottom of the reservoir was growing, however slowly.

Hacksaw could feel the water beginning to surround him. He was growing more and more anxious. From where he sat, he could see Will petting Lassie, and whispering something in her soft triangular ear.

"Forget that dog!" He yelled angrily up to Will. "I'm the one who is hurt!"

Will ignored Hacksaw's cruel remarks. Will understood that right now, "that dog" was the only one who could save Hacksaw's life!

"Go, Lassie . . . Go!" Will commanded his dog, pointing in the direction of the main road. "Get help!"

Lassie took off with the force of a rocket! Will followed with his eyes as her brown and white body sped away from him until she was completely out of his sight. Once she was gone, Will focused all of his attention on the petrified boy at the bottom of the reservoir. "Hurry, Lassie! Hurry!" Will prayed silently.

*   *   *

Lassie was doing her best. Already the dog had run down the closed road, past the three orange traffic cones, and come to a stop at the cross street. Lassie's heart pounded with nerves and hope as her sensitive ears picked up the sound of a car coming toward the crossroad. As the car approached, Lassie jumped up and down, barking frantically in order to get the driver's attention and divert him up the closed road to the reservoir. But all of Lassie's frantic jumping and barking was to no avail. The driver ignored the collie's desperate cries and drove on.

Lassie hadn't considered how difficult it would be to get humans to understand what she wanted them to do. But Lassie wouldn't give up. Within minutes she picked up the sound of a second car coming toward her. With renewed enthusiasm Lassie ran alongside the car, trying to get the driver to follow her to Will. Unfortunately, the driver of the car did not get Lassie's message either, and he drove past, ignoring the barking collie.

Lassie was getting very frustrated. She was about to turn back and join Will when she spotted the three orange traffic cones that blocked off the street. Lassie's ears perked up and her tail wagged ever so slightly as an idea bloomed in her mind. With swift, determined motions Lassie picked up the first of the three cones in

her strong jaws and dragged it over to the side
of the road behind some shrubbery. One by one
she dragged all three cones away from the road
and hid them behind the thick shrubs. When the
last cone, the one with the ROAD CLOSED warning
sign around it, was out of the way, the wise collie
stood quietly by the side of the road and waited
patiently for the next car to come.

Finally a red convertible came driving into
the intersection where Lassie stood watching.
The driver, having no idea that he was traveling
on a road that was closed for construction, drove
unaware up the hill toward the reservoir.

Lassie watched with a sigh of relief as the
car traveled in Will's direction. She had found
the perfect way to get help. But there wasn't
time for Lassie to be proud. Will still needed her
help. So, with her collie mouth pulled back in
a triumphant smile, Lassie followed the car up
the hill toward the reservoir, barking all the
way.

"Ruff! Ruff! RUFF!" Lassie's loud barks
rang out sharp and loud in the crisp fall air as
she alerted Will that a car was on its way. The
sound of Lassie's barking caught Will's attention. As he turned his head in the direction of
the sound, Will spotted the red convertible coming up the slope.

"Help! Help!" Will called from his post at the flood channel. "Help! Help!"

Lassie wasn't taking any chances that the driver wouldn't hear Will's shouts. The collie bravely ran as fast as she could until she caught up with the convertible. Then, without a thought for her own safety, Lassie jumped right out in front of the car!

SCREEEECH! The driver jammed on the brakes of the car and squealed to a halt—missing the beautiful purebred collie by less than a quarter of an inch!

The driver of the convertible forced open his car door and jumped out to see if the dog was all right. When he did, he spotted Will at the top of the hill, using all his strength to hold the homemade ramp in place.

"What the . . ." the driver began, looking from the boy at the top of the hill to the frantically barking dog and back again.

"Down there, mister," Will called to the man, pointing to Hacksaw, who was by now sitting in a pool of water and crying hysterically in fear for his life.

"Oh my goodness," the driver shouted as he leaped over the chainlink fence and ran to help Hacksaw.

"It's going to be okay," Will called excitedly to Hacksaw. "Lassie got help!"

EPILOGUE

"I know . . . I know . . . when people build a fence around something, it's for a reason," Will repeated the words his father had been saying over and over again for the past hour.

The kind man who had been driving by the reservoir in his red convertible had carefully lifted Hacksaw out of the reservoir and up to safety. Then he had used his car phone to call the hospital and have them send an ambulance to help the boy. After they had carefully placed Hacksaw in the back and put his leg in a splint, the emergency rescue workers had offered Will a chance to ride in the ambulance with them, but they made it clear that Lassie had to follow behind in the red car. As much as he wanted to ride in a speeding ambulance, Will chose to ride along with his heroic and quick-thinking collie.

When Chris arrived at the hospital, he took one look at his son and gave silent prayer of thanks that Will was all right. Chris didn't say a word in the hospital about the incident, nor on the long ride home. But as soon they walked in the front door, Chris had both Will and Lassie take a seat on the living room couch. Only then did Chris begin his lecture on safety, following rules, and reading signs. Will sat quietly on the couch, fidgeting ever so slightly.

"Fences are meant to keep people out—or, in a few cases, keep people in," Chris said, making a small joke. Will wasn't sure whether to laugh or not, so he managed a small smile.

"I knew I shouldn't have gone in there, but Hacksaw kept saying it was okay . . . 'Everybody does it.' "

Chris looked at his son sternly. "Well, you'll just have to decide who you are going to listen to in life . . . Your friends or yourself. It's not an easy choice."

"Especially if you like what your friends are saying better," Will thought out loud.

"And speaking of friends," Chris continued. "You can bet the next time Hacksaw skateboards, he'll wear his helmet and pads—just like you always do."

Will looked at the floor uncomfortably. It didn't seem like a good time to tell his dad that he hadn't been wearing any protective gear either. Lassie looked at Will knowingly; she could tell he was uncomfortable.

"Ruff. Ruff," she barked quietly, urging Will to tell the truth.

"Shhhh..." Will whispered, gently pushing the dog away.

Lassie's barks and Will's motions were not lost on Chris. "Just think, you could be the one at St. John's hospital with the compound fracture of the tibia ..." Chris suggested to Will.

Will shuddered at the thought. "Uhhhh," he moaned, thinking of Hacksaw sitting at home with a cast up to his hip.

". . . Especially because you had a loose wheel on your skateboard," Chris continued.

"I'm going to tell Tim about that tomorrow at school," Will vowed.

Chris smothered a knowing grin. "It would serve him right if he got a D on that Social Studies paper," Chris said slowly.

Will's eyes opened wide. How did his father find out about that?

"What?" Will gasped.

"Well, the craziest thing happened this afternoon ... I sat down at the computer to punch up the plans for that supermarket I'm working on over on Ontario Street," Chris began, noting the guilty look that had become apparent on his son's face. "And, well, let me put it this way . . . I just hope this supermarket doesn't come out looking like an Egyptian pyramid . . . with Tim Milford's name on it!"

"Oh, no," Will moaned.

"Will, we're living in a new age now," Chris said with a half smile. "You're going to have to learn to erase your floppy discs!"

Will shrugged his shoulders and collapsed wearily into the couch. There was no sense trying to deny it—he had been caught on all counts! Even without his father saying it, Will knew it would be a long time before he would be allowed out on a skateboard again. He was sure to be grounded!

Lassie knew it, too. But unlike Will, she was thrilled. Lassie could wrestle with Will, run with Will, play fetch with Will, even watch TV with Will. Just about the only thing she couldn't do with Will was ride his skateboard. Lassie snuggled up beside Will and licked his nose with her rough pink tongue. Then she rolled over and exposed her white chest.

Will smiled as he scratched Lassie's belly. Being grounded wasn't too bad—especially if you lived in the same house with your very best friend!